Presented to

SEONAID MARY MATHESON

PRIZEWINNER IN

BOYS & GIRLS

COMPETITION

PICKERING & INGLIS LTD.   PRINTED IN GREAT BRITAIN

MICHAEL AND SALLY
AND MA-MYA

MURIEL COLLINS

LONDON
PICKERING & INGLIS LTD.

PICKERING & INGLIS LTD.

29 LUDGATE HILL, LONDON, E.C.4
26 BOTHWELL STREET, GLASGOW, C.2

Printed in Great Britain by
Lowe & Brydone (Printers) Ltd., London

CONTENTS

CHAPTER I

INTRODUCES SALLY AND MICHAEL

"MAKE haste and get up, or you'll be late for school!" mother said, as she put her head inside Michael's room.

With a sigh and a yawn, Michael stretched himself and reluctantly tumbled out of bed.

"Wish the old hols, were longer! Wish school didn't start so beastly early in the morning!" he grumbled to himself as he began shiveringly to pull on his clothes.

The first day of term was always a trial to Michael Stevens, who—sad to relate!—was somewhat lazy by nature, and much preferred to dawdle over his dressing, and linger at the breakfast table in a nice warm, comfortable room instead of having to hurry off to school on a damp, cold morning in the middle of January!

Mother and his sister Sally were already seated at the breakfast table when Michael made his appearance, and with a rather shame-faced apology he sat down and commenced to tackle his porridge.

As he had apologised for being late, mother wisely refrained from making any remark, except to remind Michael that grace had been said, so that he might say his own.

But Sally could not refrain from a sly dig at her younger brother.

5

"Late on the first day of term, Mike!" she said with a rather virtuous air, as if to imply that she herself was never guilty of such an offence!

Truth to tell, Sally hardly ever was late in the morning. She loved to get up early and help Mother in the house before starting for school. All the same, it was rather unkind of her to rub it in to Michael at that particular moment, and he answered heatedly:

"It's all very well for you to talk when you always get longer hols. than I do! It's not fair!"

For some reason or other Michael's school usually re-opened a few days before the one which his sister attended, and this was always a sore point with him.

"I think it's quite fair!" Sally said rather patronisingly.

The atmosphere seemed to be getting a trifle stormy, and mother was just going to intervene in order to prevent a quarrel when in reaching across for the marmalade Michael's arm caught his cup and sent the contents in an ugly brown stream right across the table!

"Sorry, Mum!" he cried penitently. "I never saw the beastly cup! You'll have to fine me every time I spill anything! Alan Baker's mother does; she puts the missionary box on the table, and if anyone spills anything they have to fork out something to put in it!"

"It would be pretty heavy if you had to do that!" Sally said as she jumped up to get a cloth to wipe the table.

But mother hastily interposed. "I don't like the idea at all," she said quietly.

Both the children looked at her in astonishment.

"I thought you were so keen to get money for the missionary box?" Michael said in surprise.

"So I am; but I shouldn't like to feel it was given in that way. You see, Michael, missionary work is God's work, and we ought to give willingly to Him. A fine is all very well in its proper place, but it is money which *must* be given, and sometimes it is given very unwillingly. You see what I mean?"

"Yes, I never thought of it like that," Sally said slowly. "You mean that God likes us to give to His work because we *want* to—not because we *have* to."

"Yes," said mother with a smile. "We read that in the Bible, don't we?"

Michael looked up from his plate. "Isn't there a text where it says something about 'a cheerful giver'?" he asked.

"Yes," and mother quoted the words. 'So let him give; not grudgingly or of necessity, for God loveth a cheerful giver.'

"That's it," exclaimed Michael, "it was the key text in our S.U. portion the other day. But, Mums, why must we give to missions? There's a chap at school who says his dad always says that charity begins at home, and we ought to preach to our own people first before wasting our money on the heathen in other countries."

Mother sighed. This was an old-time argument against foreign missions, and she wondered how best she could help the children to see how wrong it was.

"You've heard of the Duke of Wellington?" she said.

"Rather!" they exclaimed; and Michael added: "He was a jolly fine general!"

"Well, listen. This is a true story about him. Once someone asked him if it was any use to preach the gospel to the Hindu. Hindus are people who live in a certain part of India, and their religion is called Hinduism. The Duke asked curtly, 'What are your marching orders'? 'Oh', was the reply, 'our marching orders are definitely to preach the gospel to every creature'. 'Very well', replied the Duke with a touch of contempt in his voice that such a plain command as this could ever be questioned or disregarded, 'you must obey the command. You have nothing whatever to do with results'."

"I say, that's fine!" Michael exclaimed. "'Marching orders'. I like that!"

"Yes, and you'll find those orders in Mark's gospel, chapter sixteen, verse fifteen," mother told them.

"I shall look it up in my Bible before I forget it," Sally said eagerly.

"That's right. And talking of missions reminds me that I've been asked to let you do something rather special this afternoon."

"Oh, Mummy! What is it? Do tell me!"

Mother smiled mysteriously.

"We'll help Michael to get off to school," she said, "and then I'll tell you all about it."

CHAPTER II

GIVES SALLY A SURPRISE

I DON'T know if you have found it so, but in the Stevens family things seemed to take it into their heads to disappear completely on the first day of term! As a result, for several minutes after breakfast the air was rent with cries of distraction from Michael: "Where is my cap? Whoever's taken my scarf? Oh, Mums, have you seen my gloves?" and so on.

Mother and Sally were kept busily running hither and thither in search of the missing articles, but at last everything was discovered.

Michael set off for school at a run, and Mother and Sally sank down with sighs of relief.

"Now, Mums, before we do anything else you promised to tell me what it was I was asked to do this afternoon," Sally said eagerly.

"Well, dear, there is a missionary meeting at three o'clock, and as you are still having holidays I thought perhaps you would like to come along with me."

Sally's face fell. "Oh, -Mums! A missionary meeting! I thought you meant something much more exciting than that!"

"It's sure to be very interesting and thrilling," mother said quietly. "A lady missionary from India is going to speak, and tell us about her work."

"Yes, but the place is sure to be full of old ladies!" said Sally impatiently. "Missionary meetings always are!"

"I'm not so sure about that!" mother said with a smile. "At the last one I went to there were lots of young people. I was sorry afterwards that I hadn't taken you and Michael with me. But now listen! Tea will be provided at the meeting, and I promised Mrs. Davidson—the lady in charge—that you would help to hand it round. She is very short of helpers and was delighted at the idea!"

Sally's face brightened.

If there was one thing she enjoyed more than anything else it was the pleasure of being asked to help with the tea at any sale or meeting. There was such a sense of importance in donning a dainty frilled apron over one's frock and carrying round trays of tea and cakes! It gave one such a delicious feeling of being almost—if not quite—grown up!

"I'll come, Mums!" she cried eagerly. "I hope there'll be crowds of people at the meeting, and I do hope they'll all stay to tea!"

When Mother and Sally reached the hall it was already filling up rapidly, and Sally noticed with satisfaction that there were lots of young people, even one or two girls from her own school.

She settled down quite happily in her seat—but there were some more pleasant surprises in store.

The meeting itself was conducted in quite a different way from any that Sally had ever been to before. There were several ministers and clergymen on the platform, and one of them opened with a short, earnest prayer that God would be with them and bless their meeting.

Then everyone got up to sing a hymn, after which another minister read a short portion out of the Bible, and then the chairman introduced the speaker, whose name was Miss Molly Brown, S.R.N.

"Now, before we proceed any further with our meeting," he said with a smile, "we are going to enjoy a cup of tea: then, when we've been warmed and refreshed we can settle down all the better to listen to the thrilling story which I know our speaker has to tell us!"

Everyone looked surprised and delighted at this welcome announcement, and Sally jumped up in a flutter of excitement to don the pretty little floral apron which had been a present to her on her last birthday.

For the next half hour she went up and down the big hall carrying innumerable trays and offering tea and cakes in her best company manner!

Everyone seemed very hungry and thirsty, and some unblushingly asked for second—and even third —cups of tea!

But at last they all seemed quite satisfied, and Sally was quite glad to snatch some tea herself, and then sit down beside mother to listen to the missionary address.

Miss Molly Brown looked astonishingly young— quite as young as the sports mistress at school, Sally decided; and more than once, when she was speaking, Sally caught an unmistakable twinkle in her eye.

"I think God gives us missionaries a special sense of humour to tide us over the obstacles that we have to face," Miss Brown said with a smile, during her address.

Sally listened, entranced, as she heard of men and women and boys and girls who had been taught by the missionaries to worship the true God instead of bowing down to dreadful-looking idols, and for the first time a great longing sprang up in her heart to do something to tell those poor ignorant people about the Lord Jesus Christ.

"I wonder if I'm too young to do anything to help," Sally said to herself, and it almost seemed as though the speaker had read her thoughts, for she suddenly said:

"No one is too young to be a missionary. I'm very glad to see so many young folk here this afternoon, and I'm sure the older friends will forgive me if in closing I say a special word to the younger ones, and I'm going to start off by asking them a question: Who was the first little lady missionary that we read of in the Bible? Hands up if you can tell me!"

Miss Brown paused and looked round expectantly. "No one knows? Then I'll tell you! It was the little girl who was taken prisoner of war when the Syrians invaded the land of Israel—we read about her in the fifth chapter of the second book of Kings. I'm sure you all know the story, but I'll just run through it to refresh your memories."

CHAPTER III

TELLS OF A GOOD RESOLVE

SALLY looked up eagerly as Miss Brown continued: "Naaman, if you remember, was the
great general of the Syrian army, and a very
important man indeed; but—he was suffering from
the terrible disease of leprosy."

Miss Brown related briefly and graphically how
the little maid told her mistress of the great prophet
Elisha, who lived in the land of Israel, and who had
power to heal Naaman of his leprosy, and how the
great general believed what the little girl had said,
and went to Elisha and was made quite well.

"If that had been all, it would have been grand,
wouldn't it?" Miss Brown said smilingly, "but that
was not the end of the story. When Naaman saw
that he was healed he became a believer in the true
God, and promised that he would no longer worship
idols. Now, don't you agree with me that the little
captive maid was a first-rate missionary? She was
far away from her own home, in a heathen land,
but I am quite sure that she never forgot to worship
the true God, and it was through her witness that a
heathen family was brought to know Him, too. We
do not know the name of that little girl, and I am
glad that we were not told it, because it is just
possible that her name might have been the same as
yours or mine, and that would be rather wonderful,

wouldn't it? She was probably called Rachel, or Ruth, or Mary, or Esther, or Sarah—"

It was the last name which made Sally sit up with a start, for although she was nearly always called 'Sally', her real proper Christian name was Sarah, and it thrilled her to think that she might have the same name as that little captive maid of long ago!

"I wish I could help someone to know about the true God!" she said to herself wistfully, and once again it almost seemed as though Miss Brown could read the unspoken thought, for she said:

"There are lots of ways in which even young folk can help to spread the Gospel, and if anyone would like to come and have a chat with me after the meeting, we might discuss ways and means of doing it."

A closing hymn was sung, and during the last verse mother felt a gentle tug at her arm.

"I'd like to speak to Miss Brown afterwards," Sally said eagerly. "Will you come with me, Mums?"

Quite a number of people wanted to do the same thing, and Miss Brown was so besieged by eager questioners that it was quite a time before Mother and Sally could get near her. But at last their turn came.

"*You* tell her, Mums. Ask her what I can do to help," Sally said in a whisper; for now that the moment had come she was suddenly overcome with an absurd feeling of shyness!

Miss Brown soon put her at her ease. "You want to do something to help?" she asked. "Well, of course, the best way of all is by prayer. I could give you the names of some of our children so that you could pray regularly for them, and then, if you wanted to do something more, we have a scheme by which people can 'adopt' a little boy or girl. If they do this, they promise to pray for the child; to send something towards its support, and to take an interest in it generally."

"Oh, I'd love to do that!" Sally said breathlessly. "Will you let me adopt a little girl, Mums?"

Mother smiled assent.

"Well, that's just splendid!" and Miss Brown looked almost as excited as Sally herself. "I think I have the very person you would like; she is a little girl who was brought to our hospital about a year ago. Her name is Ma Mya, and she is about nine years old. I will send you all the particulars about her if you give me your address; and if you can ever spare the time to write her a little letter, I know she would love to have it. We can translate it into her own language, so that she will be able to understand it."

"Is she very ill?" asked Sally.

"She was, but she is getting better every day now and will soon be able to return home. Little Ma Mya just loves the Gospel stories and we are praying that she will really put her trust in the Lord Jesus Christ. If you decide to 'adopt' her, I will let you have news of her from time to time."

And so it was all settled, and Sally went home thrilled with the idea that she had really 'adopted' a little girl for her very own!

"I've always wanted a little sister to look after," she confided to mother on her way home. "It will almost be like having one, only I suppose she will be a little *brown* sister instead of a white one!"

Michael was inclined to throw cold water on the scheme when he heard about it.

"Don't see much sense in troubling about a kid thousands of miles away!" he said rather scornfully.

But Sally refused to listen. "I can make her things and send her presents for her birthday, and at Christmas," she told herself happily, "and it will all be terribly exciting!"

But even Sally herself could never have guessed what a wonderful thing was going to happen, all because she had decided to help a little brown-faced girl far away across the sea!

CHAPTER IV

ENDS IN AN ARGUMENT

"WELL, how did you get on at school to-day?" inquired mother at supper-time that evening.

"Oh, not too badly," replied Michael.

"Any new boys?" asked Sally.

"Yes; two or three. There is one in my form."

"What is his name and where is he living, Michael?" asked mother.

"His name's Nicholls—Howard Nicholls—and I think he's living with his grandmother. He is an orphan—lost both his parents in an air-crash or something and lives with his grandmother."

"Poor boy, you must chum up with him Michael, and we will ask him to tea; he must miss his parents terribly."

"Yes," agreed Michael, "because although Dad's away, we have got you, Mums, and you're a real brick!"

Mother smiled down at him: "Thank you, Michael, old boy," she said; "and I don't know what I should have done without you and Sally now that Daddy is away—I should have been dreadfully lonely." Then mother sighed rather wistfully. "But you know, dears, when I get a bit stronger and you two are old enough to go to Boarding School, then I want to go out and work with Daddy again; if God will allow me to do so."

Mother and father were both missionaries, but after several years of hard work in India, mother's health had broken down and she was reluctantly compelled to return to England.

Michael and Sally had both been born in India, but they had been sent home when they were quite small and placed under the care of a kindly aunt. But even though Aunt Mary did all she could for them, it was not quite the same as having Mother at home, so you can imagine how overjoyed they were to have her back again.

Of course, Daddy missed them all dreadfully, but he knew that God had called him to the Mission Field, and that his place was there, and so he remained at his post.

"We've got a new master this term," continued Michael. "He seems quite decent, he's just come back from Africa. Got knocked up with the beastly climate or something, and had to come home."

Having volunteered this information, Michael settled down to finish his homework before going to bed.

A few days later he came home from school full of excitement.

"No end of a lark to-day!" he cried. "We had a thundering great argument about missions, and the end of it was that Mr. Donaldson—that's the new master—has invited us all to a Missionary Brains Trust on Saturday afternoon!

"He happened to be passing through the playground when we were arguing and he stopped to know what it was all about!

"'I say, you chaps look as though you're having a pretty heated discussion!' he said. 'What's it all about?'

"Nobody said anything, and then Nicholls blurted out:

"'It's about missions, sir; whether it's right to send missionaries abroad to the heathen.'

"'Oh, that's the trouble, is it?' Old Don exclaimed, and then he added something about it being an age-old problem. Then he laughed and said: 'Isn't it a bit chilly to stand out here in the playground discussing such an important question? Now look here, I've an idea! What do you say to having a kind of Missionary Brains Trust meeting, and then we can all air our views?'

"Of course, we all shouted 'Yes!' and Old Don looked as pleased as Punch!

"'Well, will Saturday afternoon at three o'clock suit you?' he asked. 'Right! then, be sure you all turn up, and bring any other fellows along who would like to join the discussion. I'll get the Head's permission to use our class-room'."

CHAPTER V

TELLS OF A MISSIONARY BRAINS TRUST

NEWS of the Missionary Brains Trust soon spread through the school, so that quite a number of boys, besides those who had taken part in the argument, found their way to the meeting on Saturday afternoon.

"Flop down anywhere, and make yourselves at home!" advised Mr. Donaldson, "and let's start off with the question as to whether or not we should send missionaries abroad to preach the gospel. What has anyone to say on the subject?"

There was a good deal of fidgeting and murmuring amongst the boys, but no one seemed eager to be the first to speak.

"Come on! Out with it!" urged Mr. Donaldson; and thus encouraged, Clements murmured:

"I think it would be a jolly sight better if preachers stayed at home and left the heathen alone, sir!"

"That's how you feel about it," Mr. Donaldson said quietly. "Do any of you other chaps think the same?"

Clements looked round in search of supporters, and, to his relief, two or three boys murmured a feeble assent.

"Thank you," said Mr. Donaldson. "Now, having made that our starting point, shall we go a bit

farther, and ask ourselves the reason for h
point of view?"

All eyes instinctively turned towards Cle
though expecting him to answer the challe
somehow he found it very difficult to give a con-
vincing reason for his views. At last, with rather a
touch of defiance in his voice, he said: "Well, sir,
surely there are plenty of people to convert in
England without sending fellows abroad to waste
their time over the heathen?"

"You're right on one point, Clements," Mr.
Donaldson said gravely. "There are plenty of un-
converted folk in our own land, and the need for
workers is great. Even so, do you consider that is
sufficient reason for denying the News of Salvation
to those who, in many cases, have never even had a
chance of hearing it?"

"The heathen have their own religions!" muttered
Clements: "Dad always says they're quite happy, so
why go and upset them by teaching them something
else?"

"I'm glad you've raised that question, Clements,"
Mr. Donaldson said quietly, "because I know that it
is often used as an argument against missions; but
if we are quite honest with ourselves I think we shall
be bound to admit that this argument is both
unreasonable and untrue. In the first place, very
few, if any, heathen religions have any element of
joy in them. They are religions of fear rather than of
love; and, secondly, when we know something
infinitely better—something that tells of the only

true God—what right have we to withhold that knowledge from those who do not know it?"

There was a pause, and the master continued: "Let me put it another way. Supposing you knew a great many people who were suffering from some deadly disease, and you heard of a wonderful remedy that would completely cure them. Would you say to yourself, 'I shan't bother to tell them about that remedy; they're quite happy as they are'?"

There was a murmur of indignation amongst the boys, and one, bolder than the rest, exclaimed: "Anyone who did that would be an out-and-out rotter, sir!"

"Exactly," agreed Mr. Donaldson, "and yet the Lord Jesus Christ is the only One Who can cure the disease of sin, and what right have we to withhold this knowledge from those 'other sheep' for whom He died, and who are still outside His fold?"

To most of the boys this was an entirely new thought. They were silent until Mr. Donaldson said quietly: "Has anyone anything else to say?"

"I think we ought to preach the Gospel to the heathen, sir," said Michael. "But then my parents are missionaries, so perhaps my opinion won't count for much."

"Of course it will, Stevens," said Mr. Donaldson.

"And now I'm going to ask you another question, though I'm afraid this is more like a quiz than a Brains Trust! What sort of people do you think we should be if no one had brought the Gospel to our shores?"

"Never thought!" murmured one boy: "Savages, I suppose, sir, or else kind of Red Indian scalp-hunters!"

"Exactly! Or I suppose by now we should be fairly civilised; but civilisation and education *without Christianity* can be terribly dangerous, as you will see for yourselves when you are a bit older. But now, shall we remind ourselves of our Lord's last command—'Go ye into all the world and preach the Gospel to every creature'? Surely that settles the question once and for all?"

Michael looked up eagerly at Mr. Donaldson's words, and presently, in rather a shaky voice, he found himself blurting out the story of the Duke of Wellington, which Mother had told him.

"Marching Orders! That's a fine way of putting it, Stevens, and just exactly what it means! Christ is our Captain; He has given us our Marching Orders and we must not—dare not—disobey them!"

A dreamy look stole into the young man's face; then, rousing himself, he said with a twinkle in his eye: "And now I'm going to tell you something which I think will take you all completely by surprise!"

CHAPTER VI

ENDS IN A DISASTER

THERE was a moment's pause whilst all the boys looked up expectantly. Then with a gleam of amusement in his eyes, Mr. Donaldson said quietly: "I don't suppose any of you know it, but I have been a missionary myself in West Africa, and only came home because my health broke down."

There was a murmur of surprise amongst the boys, and one or two of them exclaimed: "Who would have thought it?"

"I thought perhaps you'd say that, but wait a bit till I tell you something else. When I was your age I simply hated everything to do with foreign missions, and never dreamt of going to a missionary meeting or putting my pocket money into the missionary box. And then"—Mr. Donaldson lowered his voice—"something happened—something which changed my whole outlook on life. I realised for the first time that Jesus Christ had died for *me*, and that He was waiting for me to hand over my life to Him. And then, when I had done that, I realised that He had died for the people of India and China and Africa as well, and I determined that if the way opened I would go abroad as a missionary when I grew up. Well, the way did open, and I heard God's voice calling me to go to West Africa and tell the people there about Him."

Mr. Donaldson paused; then he said quietly: "I'm not going to preach to you chaps, but I want to say one thing, and it's this: you will never feel the necessity of missionary work until you first realise your own need of a Saviour. I wonder how many of you have faced up to this and realised the claims of Jesus Christ upon your own hearts and lives?"

Some of the boys fidgeted uneasily. Over and over again they had heard how God had sent His Son to die for the world, but somehow it had never come home to them that Jesus Christ had given His life for each of them individually, and that He wanted them to love and serve Him in return.

Many of the boys had thought of Christianity as something rather 'soft'—something that was 'all right for girls—but a fellow wanted something a bit more manly'. And yet they were bound to admit that there was nothing 'soft' or goody-goody about Mr. Donaldson. He was as manly and full of fun as any boy could wish.

Michael had listened to the young master with rather mixed feelings. He knew that both his parents were Christians, and he and Sally had been taught to say their prayers and read their Bibles; but although Michael had often been asked if he had ever invited the Lord Jesus Christ to come into his heart, somehow he had always managed to wriggle out of the question. Now, as he looked at Mr. Donaldson's glowing face, something stirred in his heart—something that made him long to have the Lord Jesus as his Saviour and Friend!

"Christ is our Captain. He has given us our marching orders, and we must not—dare not—disobey them!"

The words echoed and re-echoed through Michael's brain. How fine it would be to serve under such a Captain as that, he thought to himself.

The boys did not say much—boys never do—but Mr. Donaldson's simple, earnest words had made a deep impression upon them all, and almost unconsciously there sprang up in their hearts a tremendous admiration for the young master.

Clements alone, for some unknown reason, seemed to have taken an unreasonable dislike to him, but it was not long before even his prejudices were swept away.

Some months had gone by. It was a glorious afternoon in spring, and the boys in Michael's form had set out for a nature ramble with Mr. Donaldson.

Knowing a good deal about boyish natures, Mr. Donaldson had chosen a walk by the river, which greatly added to its attraction in the eyes of the boys, who raced hither and thither, throwing sticks and stones into the water, or peering into its depths in search of any stray fish that might be lurking therein!

The river was broad and deep, and on either side there were tall trees whose branches drooped gracefully over the water's edge.

Presently, Clements, who was a little ahead of the other boys, espied a particularly inviting-looking tree, and without waiting to ask permission he darted forward and began to climb up into its branches.

What fun it was to swing himself from bough to bough and to look down over the swirling water beneath! It was almost as good as being on board ship, he thought to himself! And then Mr. Donaldson's voice threatened to put an end to his enjoyment!

"Clements! Get down at once! That tree is not strong enough to bear you!"

The tone was imperative, and it brought an ugly frown to Clements' face.

"Just like Old Don to spoil my fun!" he muttered angrily to himself. "Shan't take any notice! Pretend I don't hear!" And he continued to swing backwards and forwards more vigorously than before.

And then—quite suddenly—something awful happened!

There was an ominous sound of cracking, and creaking and Clements felt the bough on which he was swinging begin to give way beneath him!

He tried to swing himself back to safety—but it was too late!

The frail bough snapped beneath his weight, and for one awful moment Clements felt himself falling—down!—down!—down! Then there was a terrific splash, and he disappeared beneath the water!

CHAPTER VII

TELLS OF A GALLANT RESCUE

CLEMENTS was always considered to be quite a good swimmer for his age; but it is one thing to get into your bathing trunks and swim a few hundred yards in shallow water when you are staying at the seaside for your holidays, and quite another thing to find yourself suddenly plunged into deep water, dressed in all your everyday clothes, and wearing your thick school shoes which weigh you down and make your feet feel just like two great lumps of lead!

The river was at full tide, and although Clements made a desperate effort to swim to the bank, he found himself being borne farther and farther away at every moment.

"Help! Help!" he shouted.

His cries of terror brought the rest of the boys to the scene. Mr. Donaldson was already there, and without a moment's hesitation he threw off his coat and shoes and plunged into the water.

With a few rapid strokes he reached Clements' side; but the terrified boy threw himself upon the young master, almost dragging him under the water, until it looked as though, at any moment, they would both be drowned!

With difficulty Mr. Donaldson freed himself, then, turning on his back, he told Clements to do the same.

Supporting the boy with his arms and swimming with his legs only, the young man struck out for the bank.

But this additional weight made it a tremendous struggle against the strong current, and it was only by almost superhuman strength that the young master fought his way, inch by inch, back to safety. To the watching boys it seemed an age before the bank was reached, and the two dripping figures clambered out of the water.

Mr. Donaldson only waited to regain his breath before issuing an order for everyone to return as quickly as possible.

The boys were only too glad to obey, and they set off at a brisk rate, with Mr. Donaldson and Clements bringing up the rear.

They had some distance to go, and in spite of the bright sunshine there was a fresh breeze blowing up from the river, and the two dripping figures began to shiver in their wet clothes.

Clements was a tough boy, and after a hot bath and something warm to drink, he was none the worse for his adventure. But the shock of the icy water and the effect of remaining for so long in his wet clothes, gave Mr. Donaldson a severe chill, which brought on an attack of malaria.

Malaria, as perhaps you know, is a horrid kind of fever which people get when they live in damp, swampy places, and Mr. Donaldson had suffered greatly from it whilst working as a missionary in West Africa. It was really because of this that he had been compelled to give up his work; and even now, any sudden chill was likely to bring on another attack.

For days poor Mr. Donaldson was obliged to stay in bed, and when at length he returned to his work even the most unobservant of the boys could not fail to see how ill he looked.

Clements did not say much, beyond apologising deeply for what he had done and thanking Mr. Donaldson whole-heartedly for having saved his life, but deep down in his boyish heart there sprang up a real desire to be like the young master.

Clements knew what it was that had made Mr. Donaldson brave and strong in the face of danger, for in that awful moment, when they had both been struggling in the water, Clements had seen the young master's lips move in a wordless cry for help, and he knew what that meant.

As he thought about it afterwards something stirred in Clements' heart—something which made him long to serve under Mr. Donaldson's Captain; but he crushed down the thought, telling himself that he would never be 'pi' on any account.

Somebody else was profoundly grateful to Mr. Donaldson for what he had done, and that was Clements' father. A real friendship sprang up between the two men, and Mr. Clements, who had always said he would have nothing whatever to do with foreign missions, gradually found his objections melting away as he listened, and talked, to Mr. Donaldson on the subject.

And now, before I finish this chapter, I want to tell you something about Sally.

It was only a few weeks to her birthday, so mother had asked if there was anything special that she would like for a present, and Sally found it terribly difficult to decide!

There was that new school story she wanted so badly to read—and the shiny red handbag in Mason's window which would make her feel *so* grown-up—and the fountain pen which would be so useful at school! Oh, it *was* hard to make up one's mind!

Sally's thoughts were still running on books and bags and pens, when there was a loud rat-tat at the door, and a letter fell into the box!

"For me!" cried Sally as she drew it out and tore open the envelope with trembling fingers.

Something fell out of the letter, and as Sally picked it up her face flushed with excitement.

Then, as she read through the letter, a light broke over her face.

"I know now just what I want for my birthday!" she said to herself. "Oh, I do hope Mummy will let me have it!"

CHAPTER VIII

SEES A PHOTOGRAPH TAKEN

WITH the letter clasped tightly in her hand, Sally rushed headlong into the room where Mother was sitting.

"Look, Mums!" she cried eagerly. "Miss Brown has written at last, and it's all about Ma Mya! And —oh, Mums look at this!"

Sally held up a photograph of a little smiling dark-faced girl.

"Doesn't she look sweet? And, Mums, she wants to have a photograph of *me!* Miss Brown says she has asked for a 'likeness' of the young 'Missy Sahib' who has been so kind to her! What does 'Missy Sahib' mean, Mummy?"

"It means little lady, or little Mistress," Mother said with a smile. "Well, Sally, you must try and find a photograph to send her."

"Oh, Mummy, that's just what I want to ask you about! Please may I have a photograph taken for my birthday present?"

Mother looked rather surprised. "Haven't you an old one you could send, dear?"

"Oh, no Mummy. I haven't been taken for ever such a long time—I've only got that little snap that we had taken at school, and you said yourself it wasn't a bit like me!"

Mother sighed. Then she said slowly: "Photographs cost a good deal of money these days, Sally, so I am afraid, if you decided to have one, it would have to be instead of any other present."

Just for a moment Sally wavered, as she thought of all those other things that she wanted so badly. Then she resolutely put them all out of her mind! Ma Mya had asked for a photograph, and she should have it all costs!

"I'd rather have a photograph than anything else, please!" Sally said resolutely.

"Well, dear, you shall have it. We'll go to the photographer and make the appointment straight away!"

I don't know if you like being photographed, but as a rule Sally hated the very idea! She used to say it was almost as bad as a visit to the dentist!

To begin with, it meant putting on one's best frock—not that Sally minded this, because she liked wearing pretty clothes! And then one's hair had to be made extra tidy, but it was when one reached the photographer's studio that the real ordeal began!

"Take a seat, madam" (this to Mother). "And now, missie, will you sit here, please?"

A chair was brought forward and Sally sat down, trying her hardest not to look awkward and self-conscious.

Meanwhile, having posed his 'victim' to his own satisfaction, the photographer became absorbed in the intricacies of his camera! Sometimes this lasted for so long a time that Sally's thoughts blissfully wandered away, sternly recalled by the voice of the photographer remarking blandly: "Look this way, please—a little to the left—chin a shade higher—smile a little more pronounced—ah! that's got it!"

Sally relaxed with a sigh of relief, but the operation was by no means over!

"I'd like to take another, if you don't mind. This time we'll have it a little larger!"

The camera was brought nearer while the whole process was repeated at length.

But even this was not the end!

"Just one more, please! Perhaps you would like a full-length one this time?"—with a questioning glance at Mother. "Right; then will you stand here, please, with your hand on the arm of the chair. Try not to grip it—let it just rest lightly—yes, that's better! Now turn your head a little this way, please. One foot slightly in front of the other—the head a little up—the lips a wee bit open! Ah! that's lovely! Now I need not trouble you any more!"

At last it was over, and poor Sally heaved a sigh of relief as she got up to put on her hat and coat.

A few days later an exciting-looking parcel arrived for mother with the name of the photographer printed in large letters on the label outside. This package contained the three photographs.

"These are called the 'proofs'," said Mother. "We can choose which one we like best."

It was great fun looking at them, but very hard to decide which was really the best. Mother thought the first one was very good, Sally liked the second, and Michael declared the third was quite the best of all!

There was a good deal of talk and laughter about the matter, but at last one was chosen, and Mother packed up the parcel and sent it back to the photographer with a little note, telling him which photograph they had decided to have and how many copies they wanted.

CHAPTER IX

BRINGS MICHAEL UP WITH A JERK!

MICHAEL and Sally were both working hard at school, but in spite of this life seemed full of pleasant interests and surprises.

Sally was looking forward to her birthday, when Mother had promised that she should have a party and ask some of her schoolfellows to tea and games. Then there was the ever-increasing interest of her little Indian protégée and the exciting thought of sending her the photograph of herself.

Michael, too, found plenty to interest him. His friendship with Howard Nicholls had increased, especially when the two boys had discovered that they both shared the same enthusiasm for stamp collecting.

Michael was a keen philatelist (which is really the proper name for a stamp collector, though it always seems to me far too grand a word to use!), and he had a fine collection of stamps. He used to say that it was the one thing he could boast about to Valentine Clements.

"Clements is always swanking about what he's got!" Michael would say disdainfully: "His pater's got tons of money, and he gives Clements everything he wants! He's mad on stamps, too, but he hasn't got anything like the ones I've got! He'd give anything to have them, and the other day he had the cheek to ask me if I'd sell them, and said he'd give me five pounds for the lot! Catch me selling my treasures! I wouldn't part with them for anything!"

Then, besides stamp collecting, there was something else which interested Michael very much. One day he came home from school with the information that Mr. Donaldson was giving a lecture one evening on his work in the mission field, and that it was to be illustrated by slides which had been made from his own photographs.

"Old Don wants all the boys to come, and to bring their parents and friends with them," Michael said to Mother; so she and Sally decided to go with him to the lecture.

Michael sat with rapt attention as Mr. Donaldson showed pictures of his work in West Africa, and spoke about the great need of workers to go out and tell the natives of the Saviour's love.

There was a touch of sadness in the young master's voice as he told how his health would not allow him to go back to the work which he loved so much.

"Perhaps some of you young folk will hear the call when you are a little older," he said, "and in the meantime there is plenty that you can do to help."

Ever since that afternoon at the Missionary Quiz when Mr. Donaldson had pleaded with the boys to give their hearts and lives to the Lord Jesus Christ, those words of the young man's had echoed and re-echoed through Michael's mind—"Christ is our Captain; He has given us our marching orders and we must not—dare not—disobey them."

Could Michael honestly say that Christ was his Captain? He felt sure, somehow, that Howard Nicholls could. Not that he ever talked 'pi', or thought himself better than the other chaps, but there was something about him—Michael couldn't explain it, even to himself—but there was something which made Michael long to be like him. He would have liked to talk to Mother about it, but somehow he felt very shy, and so Michael did the best thing he could have done; one night, as he was saying his prayers, he just told the Lord Jesus that he wanted Him to be his Captain, and though he could not explain it, Michael knew that Jesus *had* heard him, and come into his heart, and it gave him such a wonderful sense of happiness!

So now, as he sat and listened to Mr. Donaldson, a sudden·desire sprang up in Michael's heart to do something to help people in West Africa to learn about Jesus Christ.

He was too young yet to go out as a missionary, like his parents, but Mr. Donaldson had said that there were other ways of helping—by prayer and gifts. And the young master had reminded them of the little boy we read about in the Bible, who had the five loaves and two fishes, and how he had given them all up to Jesus to help Him to feed that great company of hungry people.

"Perhaps Jesus is waiting for you to give Him a gift that will really cost you something," Mr. Donaldson had said. "Think it over, pray over it." And Michael did.

He was very silent on the way home from the lecture. Sally chattered excitedly about the lovely pictures, but Michael was strangely quiet. He was thinking desperately hard about what he could give to help to send out missionaries to West Africa, and to other places where the people did not know about Jesus—and he was still thinking about it when Mother tucked him up in bed and gave him his good-night kiss.

As a rule Michael fell asleep as soon as his head touched the pillow, but that night he tossed and turned wakefully for a long time.

The thought of that little boy giving up all that he had to Jesus kept coming into his mind, and he longed to do the same.

But what could he give?

Michael turned the matter over in his head, and then quite suddenly—so suddenly that it almost took away his breath—an idea flashed into his mind! It was almost as though a voice had spoken to him, and yet there was no one in the room.

Michael sat up with a start and stared out into the moonlight. Then suddenly he spoke his thoughts aloud. "I'll give anything else in the world," he said slowly and deliberately, "but I couldn't—I simply couldn't!—do *that!*"

CHAPTER X

GIVES CLEMENTS A SURPRISE

THE precious photograph had been packed off to India with a little note to Ma Mya, and now Sally was saving up her pocket money to buy a Testament in one of the Indian dialects so that the little girl would be able to read God's Word in her own language.

"Ma Mya is not yet a Christian," Miss Brown had told Sally, "but she is always most interested in Bible stories, and very eager to have a Testament of her own so that she can read some of the stories for herself. Pray for her, that she may learn to love the Lord Jesus Christ."

"I do pray for her," Sally said shyly, "Oh, Mums, wouldn't it be lovely if she became a Christian?"

"Yes, darling," Mother said; "I'm so glad my girlie prays for her; it's lovely to pray that others may learn to love and follow Jesus, but first of all we must be quite sure that we really belong to Him ourselves. Sally, darling, I have often wondered if you have ever asked Jesus to come into your heart?"

Sally was silent. Of course, she went to church on Sunday and read her Bible, and said her prayers, but she never remembered having asked the Lord Jesus to come into her heart and wash away her sins.

If she had done this, Sally felt sure that it would have made a big difference in her life. She would not have been so ready to quarrel with Michael; she would have been kinder and more unselfish, and not so eager to have everything her own way. Yes, Sally knew quite well that there were lots of things in her own life which needed putting right, and yet somehow she had never faced up to it, and told Jesus about them. And now Mother had reminded her that before we pray for anyone else we ought to make quite sure we belong to Him ourselves.

It was a new and rather startling thought to Sally. Up to the present she had not thought very much about her need of a Saviour, but now, for the first time, she realised that she was a sinner in the sight of God.

Sally was terribly eager for Ma Mya to become a Christian, but even more than this Sally wanted to feel quite sure that she was really a Christian herself.

"Oh God, save me; Lord Jesus, come into my heart and make me a real Christian!" Sally said earnestly; and she was quite sure that God had heard and answered her prayer, because such a warm glow of happiness suddenly flooded her heart.

She wanted to tell everyone about it—and yet she felt terribly shy, just like she had done when she had to stand up at school on prize-giving day and recite a piece of poetry.

"I'll tell Mummy, anyhow," she said to herself, and so, when Mother went to bid her good-night, Sally put her arms round Mother's neck and told her all about it.

"Thank God!" said Mother as she kissed Sally

and held her close. "Oh, my darling, how terribly glad Daddy will be as well."

And now let us take another peep at Michael.

You remember, how he had been racking his brains to think of something that he could give to help to send out missionaries to teach the people in other lands about Jesus Christ.

There was his weekly pocket money—but that wasn't much. Then there was the ten shillings he had in the Savings Bank. And then, like a flash, Michael suddenly remembered—his stamps!—and with the thought there came the remembrance of Clements' words—"I'll give you five pounds for the lot if you'll sell them!"

Sell his stamps! Michael said to himself, almost fiercely; and yet all the time he knew that he ought to be willing to do so.

Michael lay down again, but he was far too agitated in mind to sleep. The thought of that other little boy who had given up all his loaves and fishes to Jesus kept coming into his mind in a very disturbing way.

Michael had asked Jesus to be his Captain—he had promised to serve and obey Him, and yet he was not willing to give Him his best.

Mr. Donaldson had said that money was needed desperately badly to carry on missionary work—five pounds was quite a big sum—it would help towards sending somebody to tell other people about Jesus.

There was a terrific struggle going on in Michael's heart. One minute he had quite made up his mind to part with his treasured stamps—the next minute he decided that he could never make such a sacrifice!

"Marching Orders!" The words suddenly came to his mind and Michael instinctively sat up and straightened himself. "If they're my marching orders, then I'll carry them out!" he said to himself; and then, with a little sigh, he lay down and closed his eyes.

Michael was unusually quiet at breakfast the next morning, and when he set off for school there was a flat paper parcel tucked securely under his arm. Viewed in the cold light of day, it seemed harder than ever to part with his treasures, but Michael determined to make the transaction before his resolution weakened.

"I say, Clements," he said, "are you still keen to buy my stamp collection?"

Clements paused on his way across the playground and looked at Michael with some surprise.

"Of course I am!" he said; "but I thought nothing on earth would make you part with your stamps!"

"I've changed my mind," Michael said steadily. "You can have them all if you give me the five pounds that you offered."

"Oh, you can have the money all right," Clements said airily; "I'll bring it along to school with me this afternoon." Then something in Michael's expression checked him. "I say, what's made you change your mind all of a sudden, Stevens? Are you in debt, or 'broke', or what?"

Michael hesitated. "Do you really want to know?" he asked.

"Of course I do! Out with it!"

Michael's heart was beating uncomfortably fast, but he stood his ground and looked Clements full in the face.

"I don't suppose you'll understand," he said slowly, "and you're sure to call me a perfect ass— but—I'll tell you all the same!"

CHAPTER XI

IN WHICH MICHAEL SPEAKS OUT

ONCE again Michael hesitated, as though he found it desperately hard to speak; then, with a swift prayer for courage, he said quietly: "My Captain needed the money for His work, and my Marching Orders are to give it to Him."

"Marching Orders! What on earth are you talking about? And who do you mean by your Captain?" exclaimed Clements.

"My Captain is the Lord Jesus Christ!" said Michael bravely, "and my 'Marching Orders' are to go into all the world and preach the Gospel to every creature. I can't go myself—not yet, anyway—but I can help to send someone else, and that's what I want the five pounds for."

Then, as though he could not trust himself to say more, Michael turned abruptly aside and almost ran into the arms of Mr. Donaldson!

"I say! I'm awfully sorry, sir!" he stammered. "I wasn't looking where I was going!" And Michael made good his escape.

Clements had already torn open the parcel and was gloating over the carefully-arranged collection.

"Aren't they beauties, sir? I've just bought them from Stevens. He's got a jolly fine collection!"

"Stevens!" echoed Mr. Donaldson. "I thought

he was so proud of his stamps. What made him want to sell them, I wonder?"

"Oh, some rot about 'Marching Orders' and giving the money to his Captain!" Clements said in rather a sneering way.

A light broke over Mr. Donaldson's face. "It's not rot, Clements," he said gravely, "it's a jolly fine thing to have done. Stevens thought no end of his stamps, I know, and it must have been a real wrench for him to part with them. I doubt if I would have made such a sacrifice," the young man added below his breath.

Michael had rather dreaded the thought of going home without his precious book of stamps, but although he was human enough to feel a pang of regret whenever he thought of his lost treasures, above all this there was such an overwhelming sense of happiness in his heart that more than compensated him for the sacrifice he had made.

When he got back from school Michael found Sally immersed in a book about missionary work in India which she had borrowed from the public library.

"I want to learn all I can about the native people," Sally said, "and the way they live, so that I can understand more about little Ma Mya. And oh, Mums, there's such a lovely piece of poetry in this book! Shall I read it to you?"

"Yes, darling, I should like to hear the poem," Mother said. And this is what Sally read:

Little Brown Sister, across the sea,
Jesus loves you just as much as me,
Little Brown Sister, I wish you knew
Jesus, my Saviour, has died for you.

Little Brown Sister, so far away,
When I kneel down every day to pray,
I shall ask Jesus to care for you—
He will do all that we ask Him to.

Little Brown Sister, I want to be—
When I'm grown up—a missionary,
So as to tell little girls like you
They have a Saviour Who loves them, too!

The verses seemed to express just exactly what Sally felt about little Ma Mya.

She did so long for her to become a Christian, and she used to pray every day that the little Indian girl might really learn to love the Lord Jesus Christ, and since she had begun to take an interest in Missionary work a dawning hope had sprung up in Sally's heart that one day—when she was older— she might even be able to go abroad herself as a missionary, to tell little girls and big girls how Jesus loved them and had died for them. Since that night when Sally had asked the Lord Jesus Christ into her heart she felt that she could really pray for anything she wanted, and she felt sure that God would hear and answer her prayers.

"I'm just longing for the next letter from India!" she said repeatedly. "I do want to hear if Ma Mya likes my photograph!"

CHAPTER XII

TELLS OF A DISAPPOINTMENT

DADDY used to write to Mummy regularly by air mail every week, and usually the letter would come by the first post on Tuesday morning.

Of course, Daddy wrote quite often to the children as well, especially on their Birthdays, or at Christmas, or on any other special occasion, but Mummy's letter came with unfailing regularity and she always wrote back to Daddy on the same day, so that he would get a letter from home every week as well.

Sally, as I told you in the first chapter (though I expect you have forgotten!) was always up early, and she liked to get downstairs before anyone else to take in the letters, when she heard the postman's knock! But on this particular Tuesday morning there was no letter from Daddy.

There was only a circular, an uninteresting-looking unsealed envelope, which looked very much as though it only contained a bill, and a postcard for Michael. Sally carried them into the living-room where Mummy was already laying the table for breakfast.

"A letter from Daddy?" Mummy said eagerly.

"Not to-day, Mums, I'm afraid." Sally tried to speak cheerfully, but she hated to see the look of disappointment which came into Mummy's face as it always did when the letter from Daddy did not arrive at the usual time.

"Perhaps it will come by the second post," suggested Michael, as he came into the room at that moment—"it does sometimes you know—and, by the way, don't forget to let me have the Indian stamp will you to start off my collection again?"

Mother nodded assent. "Of course you shall Michael, and you can have the Canadian one from the letter which I got from my cousin in Canada yesterday."

"Thanks ever so much Mums—I'll soon have a good collection again. Old Don—beg his pardon(!) —Mr. Donaldson, has promised me some African stamps. He's got quite a lot as the people from the Mission Station where he worked still write to him."

Mother smiled very tenderly at Michael. She knew what a real sacrifice he had made in parting with his cherished stamps in order to send out money to help on Missionary work, and she knew that God would bless and reward him in a special way.

"And now you must come along to breakfast, or you'll be late for school," admonished Mother. "And I don't want you both to get a black mark for unpunctuality!"

"Goodbye Mums!" Sally said later, as she started off for school. "Don't worry about Daddy, perhaps there'll be a letter—as Michael suggested by the second post."

But there was no letter from Daddy when Sally and Michael came home to dinner. "Never mind, I expect it will come to-morrow," Mother said hope-fully; but it didn't. Wednesday came and Thursday and then Friday, but there was still no letter written on the thin blue paper in the envelope with the foreign stamp which the children knew so well by sight. Mother tried not to look too troubled, but Sally, and even Michael, realised that she was worried over not having heard from father at the usual time.

"It's the first time his letter has been so late in coming," mother said on Friday at breakfast time. "If there's nothing by to-morrow's post I almost think I had better send a cable just to see if every-thing is all right."

"But doesn't that cost a lot of money!" exclaimed Michael.

"Yes, I'm afraid it would be rather expensive," Mother sighed, "but I feel a little worried about not hearing from Daddy—in these troublous times one never knows quite what is happening. Well, we must just hope and trust, my darlings, that all is well, only don't forget to pray for Daddy when you say your prayers."

"As if we would!" both Michael and Sally ex-claimed almost indignantly.

"I pray for him every night and morning," Sally said rather shyly, while Michael nodded his head to show that he did the same.

"Of course I know you do, my darlings, but put up a special prayer that God will keep him quite safe and well . . . and"—Mother paused—"if it is

God's will we may have news from him very soon!"

That night when Sally knelt down to say her prayers at bed-time, she remembered what Mother had said and she prayed longer than usual for Daddy.

"Please, God, keep Daddy safe and well," Sally pleaded, "because we all love him so much, and please, if it is your will, let there be a letter from him very soon so that Mummy won't have to worry."

Ever since Sally had asked the Lord Jesus into her heart, prayer had become very real to her. Of course she had always said her prayers before, but somehow, she had repeated them rather mechanically— more like you might say something you had learnt off by heart for a lesson, but now, she felt that she was talking to Someone Who was really listening and Who was able and willing to answer her prayers.

And it was really amazing what answers Sally had received.

For instance there was that difficult sum that she simply *couldn't* get right—and then Sally decided to pray about it—and when she tackled it again, to her delight, she was able to do it quite simply and easily.

And then there was that time when she lost her school book and searched high and low everywhere for it and then—she remembered prayer—and almost at once Sally found it had fallen down under the table where she had been sitting.

Of course there was nothing magical about it, Sally knew perfectly well that God was not a great conjuror who did all sorts of wonderful tricks like the conjuror who had performed at her school breaking-up party last year.

No, God was a Loving Heavenly Father who loved to hear and answer His children's prayers. Sally felt now that she really belonged to Him and she could pray in confidence knowing that God would hear her prayers.

So she prayed earnestly that they might hear from Daddy very soon.

"And, please, if it is Your will, let the letter come to-morrow so that Mummy won't have to cable," Sally prayed as she scrambled into bed.

CHAPTER XIII

BRINGS BAD NEWS

THE next day was Saturday, and as it was a school holiday, breakfast was always half an hour later, so that Mother could have a little extra rest in bed.

You see, during term time it was the only chance she had of having—what Michael and Sally called—a good 'lie in'. Even on Sunday, breakfast could not be too late, for Sally and Michael both attended morning Sunday School and then joined Mother at Church for the morning service. But on Saturday there was no great rush and things could be taken more leisurely.

Michael had turned over a new leaf by getting up directly he heard Mother's knock in the morning, so that he always got off to school in good time, but I'm afraid, he did like to lie and stretch luxuriously in bed for that extra half hour on Saturday morning!

But Sally was always up with the lark, and she had made a practice of making Mother an early cup of tea and taking it up to her in bed. Sally knew that in India people drank lots and lots of tea—far more than they do in England—and she knew how Mummy missed her early cup, for of course, she had so much to do during term-time in getting the children off to school that there was no time to think of making tea for herself!

And so, during the holidays, and every Saturday morning, Sally would slip down in her dressing-gown to the kitchen, as soon as she was awake, and put on the kettle and then carry up a steaming cup of tea for mother.

Mother didn't say much, but Sally knew by her face, how much she appreciated it, and even on the coldest—and darkest—of winter mornings, when bed seemed very cosy and inviting, Sally still got up early so that Mother should not miss her early cup of tea.

On this particular Saturday Sally was down earlier than usual. It was a lovely day, the birds were singing over their morning breakfast and there was a little song of hope in Sally's heart as well. Had she not prayed that there would be a letter from Daddy to-day, and was it not up to her to believe that God had answered her prayer? Only last Sunday in Sunday School the teacher had pointed out that when we prayed, we must believe that God will answer our prayers.

"I do believe," Sally said gleefully as she skipped across to the gas stove to put on the kettle.

"Rat-a-tat-tat!"

Sally almost dropped the kettle in her excitement. She only waited for the postman's steps to die away before rushing into the hall. Then just for a minute she hesitated. Supposing God hadn't heard her prayer—supposing there wasn't a letter from Daddy after all—

"Well, God knew best—Mother always said so,

she would just go on trusting," Sally told herself
bravely and she hurried to the hall door and lifted
the flap of the letter box.

There was just one letter. Sally lifted it out with
trembling fingers—then her heart gave a great bound
of joy. There it was, the square blue envelope with
the foreign stamp. So God had heard her prayer.
"Thank you, God," she whispered as she hurried
back into the kitchenette to finish making the tea.

"Now Mummy won't be worried any more and
she won't have to cable to India," Sally told herself
joyfully.

She laid the precious letter down on the table and
then for the first time Sally noticed that there was
something different about it. Of course, that wasn't
Daddy's writing on the envelope. Sally knew his
writing quite well and it wasn't a bit like that!

Well, perhaps someone else had addressed the
envelope for him, and yet, for the first time a wee
feeling of uneasiness crept into Sally's mind.

She finished making the tea, then carried it care-
fully upstairs and knocked on Mother's door.

"Come in darling. It *is* good of you to wait on
me like this." Then Mother's eyes fell on the square
blue envelope which Sally had propped up on the
tray.

"A letter from Daddy!" she exclaimed eagerly,
sitting up in bed.

"Yes—but—" Sally was beginning, but Mother
had already taken the letter from her and was
looking at it in a puzzled way.

"This isn't Daddy's writing," she said. "Oh, I do hope he is all right," and Mother began unfolding the closely written sheet of paper.

Sally longed to wait and hear if Daddy was all right but somehow she felt that Mummy would rather read her letter first alone, so she slipped away to her own room and started dressing.

It seemed an age before she heard Mother's voice calling to her to come. Mother was still in bed, her face was very white, and Sally noticed that her tea was standing untouched on the bedside table beside her where Sally had put it.

"Oh, Mummy, your tea will be all cold," Sally exclaimed, and then realised what a stupid thing it was to say when Mummy looked so upset.

"Never mind about the tea, Sally," Mother said quietly, "but come and sit down and hear the news I've had about Daddy."

"Is it bad news, Mummy?" Sally whispered, while a little shiver of apprehension ran through her.

Mother hesitated. "I'm afraid it is rather, but we must be brave, you and I and Michael, and pray for Daddy."

"What is the matter with him?" Sally whispered.

"He has had a bad black-out and lost his memory for the time being."

Sally shivered. "But what's made him lose his memory Mummy?"

"Listen, and I'll tell you," and Mummy began reading the closely written letter.

"I won't tell you all it contained as it would take

too long, but one of Daddy's fellow missionaries had written it and he told how Daddy had suddenly and completely lost his memory! He had been out visiting in a nearby village and got back to the Mission Station very tired and then after having had his evening meal he just wandered out on to the verandah and asked where he was! His fellow missionaries could see that something was wrong, so they sent off to the nearest doctor who was some miles away, and asked him to come as soon as possible. When he saw Daddy, he said that he had been overworking and must have complete rest, so he made arrangements for him to be taken to the nearest Mission Hospital where this particular doctor happened to be working himself. The letter went on to say that it would not be advisable to send Daddy home in his present state, as it was necessary for him to have perfect rest and quiet in order to help him to regain his memory.

"I think I ought to go out to him," Mother said anxiously: "I can't bear to think of him lying there ill and all alone and perhaps if he saw me it would help him to regain his memory. Oh, Sally darling, pray hard, pray that we may be guided what to do, and pray that Daddy's memory may come back to him again."

When Michael heard the news, he tried his best to act the comforter. "Don't worry too much, Mums," he said awkwardly.

"I expect Daddy will get all right, if he has a good rest,"

Mother smiled wanly. "I feel I must go to him," she said. "I'm sure Auntie Mary would come and look after you if I explained it to her."

The next day there was a long letter from the Secretary of the Missionary Society under which Daddy worked.

It was such a kind letter, and the Secretary had even thought of sending a little money to Mother in case Daddy hadn't been able to let her have the usual allowance.

He said how sorry they all were at Headquarters to hear about Daddy, and he ended by saying that if Mummy thought it would do any good if she went to see Daddy then the Society would be willing to pay half the cost of the flight out to India.

When Mummy read that she decided to go as soon as possible.

After that everything was bustle and confusion. Letters and cablegrams went backwards and forwards to different people.

Aunt Mary promised to come and keep house while Mother was away, and Mother had even booked her seat on the air liner for India when something marvellous happened!

CHAPTER XIV

ENDS IN A BIG SURPRISE

IT was early the next morning when the cablegram from India arrived.

Sally took it in and when Mother tore open the envelope and read the contents Sally thought for one awful moment that she was going to faint.

Her face went ashy white and her hands trembled, and then she put her head down on the table and actually began to cry.

Sally herself felt suddenly all sick and dizzy, just like you do before you have a bad bilious attack.

"Mummy! What is it?" she cried desperately: "Mummy! Daddy isn't *dead?*"

Mother raised her head and smiled through her tears. "Oh no, darling, Daddy is much better. He is quite well, thank God! Look darling, read the cablegram for yourself and see what it says."

There were only a few words and Sally scanned them eagerly: "Stevens fully recovered—will return home shortly. Letter follows."

A thrill of joy shot through Sally as she read the words. "Daddy's well again," she shouted at the top of her voice, waving the cablegram in the air, and at the sound Michael came hurrying in to hear what it was all about.

"Hurrah! Hurrah!" he cried as he read the cablegram. "Now you won't have to go to India, Mummy,

and Daddy's coming home! Oh, isn't it all too
smashing for words?"

"Yes," Mother said, but even as she spoke her
voice broke into a sob once again.

"Mummy! What's the matter? Aren't you well?"
exclaimed Sally.

"Yes, of course," Mother dried her eyes and
smiled at the children.

"Of course I am, my pets; it was stupid of me to
give way like that, but I suppose it was the joy of
knowing that Daddy was all right again."

Of course, grown-ups would have shaken their
heads very wisely and whispered that mysterious
word '*Reaction*', but Michael and Sally thought it
rather strange that Mother should have kept up so
bravely all the time when she was so anxious about
Daddy, and then when the news came that he was
well again, she should suddenly break down and cry!

They both looked at her in rather a puzzled way
and Mother smiled at them and wiped her eyes,
then she said: "Let's all kneel down and thank God
for His goodness to Daddy and then I must go and
cancel my seat on the air liner."

*   *   *   *   *   *

You can imagine how eagerly they all waited for
the promised letter from India and when it came it
was written by Daddy himself!

He did not say very much; only that he had completely recovered his memory, but the doctor thought
it wiser for him to come home for a period of rest
and change and so the Missionary authorities had

given him leave to take his furlough a year earlier than it was due.

"I wonder how he got back his memory?" Sally said.

"I don't know darling, he doesn't say, but he says he'll explain it all to us when he comes home."

I haven't time to tell you about all the excitement and happiness of Daddy's homecoming, but I do want to tell you what it was that made him recover his memory, because it happened in such a wonderful way.

You remember after Daddy had the black-out how he was taken to hospital with complete loss of memory, and not even knowing where he was? Very gradually things began to come back to him and he remembered going out visiting that day in the village, but his mind was a perfect blank concerning everything before that time. He could not even remember his name or where he lived or anything about Mummy or Sally or Michael! Well, the hospital to which he had been taken, happened to be the very one where Miss Brown was then working as a nurse! Of course she knew all about Daddy and all about Mummy and Sally because Sally had 'adopted' little Ma Mya, so Miss Brown tried to tell Daddy all about his home and family, but it was no use, he just could not remember anything about them at all!

Well it so ·happened that while Daddy was in hospital the precious photograph arrived from Sally for little Ma Mya. By that time Ma Mya was much better, and had gone home, but she used to come back twice a week for treatment at the hospital. Sally had addressed the parcel to Miss Brown so, when she opened it, Miss Brown put the photograph on the mantelpiece in the Dispensary, intending to give it to Ma Mya next time she came to the hospital for treatment.

"Well, Daddy was a little better by then and the doctor tried to give him light jobs to do, in the hope that perhaps this would help to restore his memory."

Well, it so happened, that very day Daddy was asked to go into the Dispensary to fetch something for the doctor, and as he went in his eyes fell on the photograph of Sally which was standing propped up on the mantelpiece.

Daddy stood quite still as though rooted to the spot, and then he put his hands to his head as though he were thinking very hard, and then suddenly he said over and over again: "My little girl! My own little Sally!"

And then slowly, but clearly, everything came back to his memory and it was all because of that photograph which Sally had sent to the little native girl of India!

You will be glad to know that Daddy got quite well and the doctors said that he was never likely to lose his memory again.

It had only happened because he had been working so hard. But the rest at home made him quite fit again and later on both he and Mother were able to return to India to the work they both loved so much.

Well, I think we have come to the end of our story now, but before I finish I must tell you one or two things of interest, and the first is about little Ma Mya herself.

You know how earnestly Sally had prayed that she might become a Christian; well, one day that prayer was answered, and the little Indian girl asked the Lord Jesus to come into her heart.

"It has made a real change in her life," Miss Brown wrote to Sally, "and now she is witnessing to her own people at home. I go to visit them from time to time and they are always pleased to welcome me. I believe soon the whole family will become Christians, so go on praying won't you?" And, of course Sally did.

And now a word about Michael.

You remember how he sold his precious stamps to his school fellow Clements so that he could give the money to Missionary work? Well, the story did not end there; whenever we give up anything for God He always gives us something far better, and this is the way that He rewarded Michael.

Clements did not say much at the time, but the very fact that Michael had been willing to part with his dearest possession and also that he had been brave enough to confess the reason as to why he had done it—all this made a deep impression on his school fellow.

Clements had plenty of physical courage but he

saw that Michael had moral courage as well, and that is something which is often rarer to find, and far harder to display.

Boys never talk much about themselves, but one day Clements told Michael enough to make him understand that he too wanted to serve under the same Captain, and that, in itself, more than compensated Michael for the loss of his stamps.

Neither Michael nor Sally could ever have expressed all that they felt, but, if their thoughts could have been written down, I think they might have been something like this:

Sally: "Ma Mya and I both love Jesus now!"

Michael· "Clements and I are both serving under the same Captain!"

Both together "Daddy is quite well again and everything's all right now!"

And if Mother and Father could have added their thoughts, I think they might have been something like this:

"Yes, God has been very good to us, we can never thank Him enough for His goodness and we are sure that Sally and Michael will have a special reward, because they have both done their best to carry out His MARCHING ORDERS!"